To HEIDI

COPPELIA

The Girl With Enamel Eyes

ADAPTED AND ILLUSTRATED BY

Warren Chappell

MUSIC BY *Léo Delibes*

COPPELIA

The Girl With Enamel Eyes

New York: Alfred·A·Knopf

L. C. Catalog card number: 65-21567

THIS IS A BORZOI BOOK, PUBLISHED BY ALFRED A. KNOPF, INC.

Copyright © 1965 by Warren Chappell

Grateful acknowledgements are made to Sam Morgenstern
who adapted the music used in this book,
and Peter March of the Tschaikovsky Foundation
who supplied the original score.

Prelude

ONCE UPON A TIME, *in far away Galicia, there lived an old man who was a stranger even to his nearest neighbors. His name was Doctor Coppélius. His daughter, Coppélia, aroused the townspeople's curiosity by sitting motionless, book in hand, day after day, at an open window of the Doctor's house on the town square.*

NOW, it happened that there was a young girl who had more reason to be curious about Coppélia than anyone else. She was the beautiful and spirited Swanilda, who suspected the doctor's daughter of being her rival. More and more often, she had noticed that her sweetheart, Franz, would stop beneath Coppélia's window to gaze up at her and try to get her attention.

Late one summer afternoon, Swanilda resolved to have a better view of this girl who never moved, never nodded in answer to a friendly greeting. "What," she thought, "can Franz find attractive in such a face, so cold and waxlike?" She went out into the square and began to dance, as if she were interested in nothing more than the joy of motion. But she designed the pattern of her dance to take her closer and closer to the house of Doctor Coppélius.

No one knew anything about this old man. Some people said

Swanhilda's Waltz

that he was an inventor. Others said he was a magician. Everyone shunned him as if he were an evil spirit.

As Swanilda's waltzing steps took her nearer to her goal, she heard the sound of someone approaching. Quickly, she ran to the side of the square and found a place to hide.

IT was Franz! He went toward Coppélia's window as if he were being drawn by a magic spell. From where she stood, Swanilda could see the shadowy figure of Doctor Coppélius standing in the semi-darkness of the alcove, behind the girl in the window. His hand was on her shoulder, and his gaze was fixed on the youth below. But Franz saw only the girl. Without making a sound, his lips formed the words, "Beautiful one, tell me that my love for you is not in vain."

Coppélia nodded to him! She laid aside her book with one hand and, with the other, made a little gesture of greeting. Her movements were stiff and awkward, but to the enchanted youth, they were lovely. He blew her a kiss. Suddenly, Doctor Coppélius drew the curtain, shutting off his daughter from view.

Swanilda had seen it all, and she was as angry as she was sad. But she did not want to be caught spying, so she ran from her hiding place and began to pursue a butterfly across the square.

Franz's Mazurka

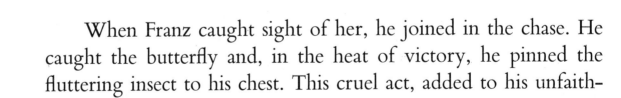

When Franz caught sight of her, he joined in the chase. He caught the butterfly and, in the heat of victory, he pinned the fluttering insect to his chest. This cruel act, added to his unfaith-

fulness, made Swanilda think her heart would break. She reproached the fickle boy bitterly, but her protests were stilled by the sound of a drum and the arrival of several people in the square.

SOON, the Burgermaster entered the square, preceded by a young drummer whose spirited rolls and tattoos had announced their coming. The pair halted, and the drummer stepped back several paces, standing at attention as the Burgermaster began to read from a large sheet of paper which he carried.

"Hear ye, hear ye. It is proclaimed that tomorrow will be a holiday, to be called the Festival of the Hours. His Excellency, the Lord of the Manor, will present a new clock to the town, and a dowry to every couple who chooses this happy occasion to be their wedding day."

Everyone thought that Franz and Swanilda would be among the ones to marry on the holiday. But when Swanilda was asked, she did not answer. Instead, she picked up a stalk of grain and held it to her ear, trusting in the old custom that said the grain would give her a message. It seemed to whisper "No!" Swanilda went to

Slavonic Dance

staccato

Franz, and snapped the stalk in two before his eyes. With that sign, their engagement was broken.

A dance began in the square, but the rejected Franz did not join in. He strode away. The dancers remained until only a trace of sunlight was in the square.

WHEN, at last, the square was dark and deserted, Doctor Coppélius came out of his house. He was dressed in a long coat, and his three-cornered hat was pulled down tightly on his head. After carefully locking the door, he cast a final upward glance toward the window where Coppélia's shadow showed against the curtain. Then, he started across the square. Immediately, as if they had come out of the air, a group of boys surrounded the old man. They teased him, shouting:

> *"Devil, devil, eats dead rats,*
> *Sleeps in bed with blind black bats!"*

Coppélius raised his stick and, with angry thrusts, succeeded in driving them off. But, in the struggle, he dropped the key to his house and, unaware, continued on his way.

Swanilda was nearby with several companions. When they heard the commotion, they ran in the direction of the sounds. The

Dance of the Dolls

square was empty, but Swanilda saw the key lying on the ground. "It is his," she said, pointing toward Doctor Coppélius' house. Picking up the key, she told her friends to follow her, and led them inside, leaving the door ajar.

A few moments later, Franz appeared, carrying a ladder. Rejected by Swanilda, he was determined to speak to Coppélia.

Suddenly, Doctor Coppélius, having discovered that his key was gone, came hurrying back to his house. He caught a glimpse of Franz, then his eye lit upon his open door. Fearing the worst, he went inside.

Dance of the Dolls
(continued)

SWANILDA and her friends had entered a dimly lighted workroom. On pedestals placed about the room stood dolls as large as life, all in fantastic dress. Worktables were cluttered with tools, instruments, and small machines that looked like clockworks. Swanilda went quickly to a curtain drawn across the end of the room, and pulled it slightly aside. There sat Coppélia in her window alcove, a book still in her hands.

"I beg your pardon," said Swanilda, ashamed of having broken in on the girl without any warning. But there was no reply. She touched the seated figure, then felt near the heart. "There is no heartbeat!" exclaimed Swanilda. "Coppélia is not a living girl. She is a doll—a doll with enamel eyes!"

Just then, one of Swanilda's friends tripped over a figure and, at once, it began to move its arms and legs to the sound of a tinkling tune. One by one, the girls wound up all the machines and set the

Dance of the Dolls
(continued)

figures in motion. The dancing dolls were weaving and swaying about when Doctor Coppélius strode into the room. The other girls managed to escape, but Swanilda was left behind in the curtained alcove—with Coppélia.

Doctor Coppélius quieted all his dolls, turning off their clockwork motions. Then, suddenly, he was aware that Franz had set up his ladder. As the boy came in through the window, Doctor Coppélius was waiting for him.

"Thief, housebreaker! What does this mean?" he shouted.

"No, no!" protested Franz. "I'm not a thief. I love your daughter, sir, and I have come to tell her so."

The Doctor pretended to be satisfied with that explanation and, in a most friendly manner, he poured two drinks, offering one to the boy. He proposed a toast, "To love!" but he did not touch his own glass, because the drinks were drugged. The trusting boy, however, drank his, and he was soon asleep. Quickly, Doctor Coppélius began to search in his dusty books for the magic words he needed. He was determined to put the life force of the foolish youth into the lifeless form of his beloved Coppélia. Believing all was ready, he wheeled the doll from her alcove.

IN his great excitement, the old doctor did not notice that the form before him was not Coppélia. It was Swanilda. While she was hiding behind the curtain, she had disguised herself as the doll. The words from the magic book were spoken by Doctor Coppélius, and the false Coppélia began to move. She rose jerkily, then she stepped from her pedestal. Doctor Coppélius was beside himself with joy. "She comes to life," he whispered, as if he feared he might break the spell.

Swanilda slowly acted out the miraculous change. She opened her eyes, and began to move about the room. She approached the sleeping Franz and shook him with all her strength. But Doctor Coppélius pulled her away, and tried to hold her interest by offering her pieces of lace and silk. It did not work. Her movements became more and more violent. She moved so wildly about the room that she overturned all the figures—and awakened her sweetheart! The old doctor, believing his spell had been broken, pushed

Coppélia's Waltz

Mouvement de valse

the girl back onto her pedestal and wheeled her behind the curtain. Then, angrily, he drove the startled youth from his house.

* * *

Doctor Coppélius did not see Swanilda escape from her hiding place down Franz's ladder. When he entered the alcove, there was his beloved Coppélia. She was standing rigidly, and her clothes were gone! Even her wig had been taken by Swanilda, who had joined Franz in the street below.

THE next day brought the promised holiday and festival. It was a happy occasion. There was much laughing and talking, eating and drinking, dancing and, of course, singing. The great new clock was presented to the town, and the couples who were to be married stood before the seated Lord of the Manor to receive their bountiful dowries. Franz had asked Swanilda to forgive him for falling in love with a clockwork doll, whose eyes were merely painted on. She had, and both of them looked so happy that they brought smiles to all the faces in the crowd.

Only Doctor Coppélius was not in a festive mood. He was bemoaning his broken figures and his wounded pride. Swanilda felt sorry for him, and she offered her dowry to help repay him. But the Lord of the Manor would not allow it. Instead, he gave the old man a generous purse, and sent him away as happy as might be hoped. And with that, there was nothing left to mar the perfect day.

Festival Dance

T H E

E N D

Mouvement de valse